To my nephews—Giancarlo, Kevin, and Aaron.
You are my heart.

www.mascotbooks.com

Ronnie Turns Fear into Fun

For more information, please contact:
Mascot Books
620 Herndon Parkway, Suite 320
Herndon, VA 20170
info@mascotbooks.com

Library of Congress Control Number: 2018904155

CPSIA Code: PRT0718A
ISBN-13: 978-1-68401-768-3

Printed in the United States

Ronnie Turns Fear into Fun

Ingrid Hoyos

Illustrated by
Ana Sebastian

Ronnie has a special talent no one knows.

She can turn a handkerchief into a rose.

She can make cups float in midair.
She can sit on an invisible chair.

Ronnie wants to be the greatest magician of all time.
She practices every day with a quarter and dime.

Abracadabra Callabazu,
Yoli Anchovee Caramel
Poof!

When it is time for the citywide talent show,
Ronnie does not think she is ready to go.

She looks to her father with worried eyes.
She has got a bad case of the butterflies.

"If only I could perform all of my tricks in front of an audience of more than six.

But I am too afraid to get up on stage.
With so many people, I feel so strange."

"I sweat and I shake and my tummy, it rumbles.
I try to speak but all I can do is mumble.

A thousand butterflies invade my belly.
My tongue twists into a pretzel and my legs turn to jelly."

"I believe in your talent," says Father Rabbit.

"There is magic within you, now it is time to share it.

Turning fear into fun is the greatest trick of them all.

You will figure it out, just stand proud and stand tall."

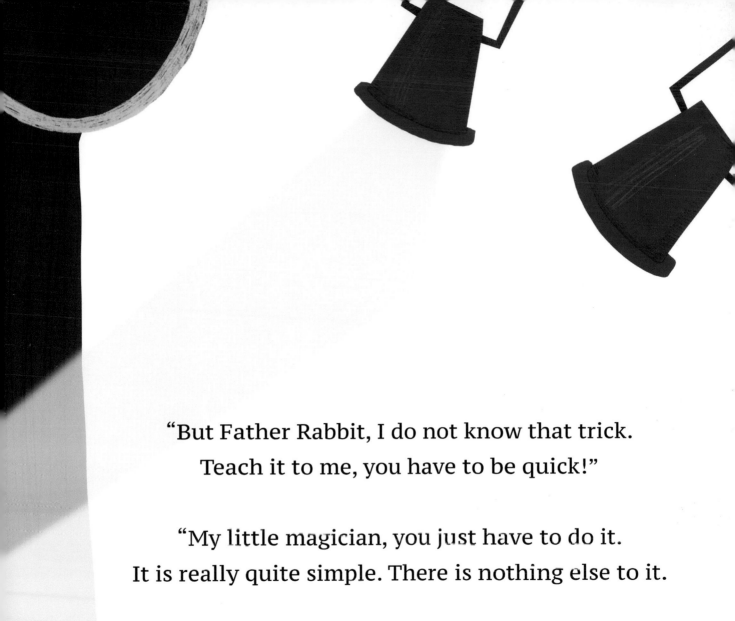

"But Father Rabbit, I do not know that trick.
Teach it to me, you have to be quick!"

"My little magician, you just have to do it.
It is really quite simple. There is nothing else to it.

Raise the red curtains, hit the bright lights.
No matter what happens, you will be alright."

So Ronnie the Rabbit went on with the show,
as scared as a cat but ready to go.

She started to speak and something great happened.

Performing was not as bad as she had imagined.

With a swish and a swash of her magic wand,
the butterflies in her stomach were gone.

Then a few magic words she began to say
and all her worrying turned into play.

She blew on a cane and made it disappear.
She pulled rainbow scarves from out of her ear.

She shuffled cards like
The Great Cardini.

She made an escape
like Harry Houdini.

For the grand finale she had a surprise.

She tapped on her hat and made butterflies rise.

Like purple confetti, they flew off the stage.
With eyes full of wonder, the audience gazed.

Ronnie could not believe it, what a treat!
She had the audience up on their feet.

They cheered and they clapped for the marvelous show.

But there was one last thing they needed to know.

As purple butterflies reached the ceiling,
her new magic trick, she started revealing.

"Turning fear into fun is something you can do too.
Just believe in yourself and your magic will shine through."

the
End

About the Author

Ingrid was born in Bogotá, Colombia, and raised in Miami Beach, Florida. She received her Bachelor of Arts degree from Florida International University and worked as a reporter and producer for *The Miami Herald*. Today, she is a writer and actor based in Los Angeles, California.

Having struggled with anxiety for many years, her childhood dreams of becoming a performer felt impossible to reach, but just like her character, Ronnie the Rabbit, she discovered that fear isn't all that bad.

Through this book, Ingrid hopes children learn that when they embrace their fears, they gain the power and confidence to accomplish anything they set their minds to.

About the Illustrator

Ana Sebastian, also known as Pebbles, is an illustrator based in the peaceful town of Zaragoza, Spain. She studied fine arts at the University of Zaragoza and the Université Michel de Montaigne, Bordeaux, specializing in illustration. Ana also earned a Master's Degree in digital illustration for concept art and visual development. She is now a freelance illustrator, working mostly on children's picture books and editorial illustrations. When she isn't drawing, Ana can be found reading, diving, traveling, watching movies, or baking something sweet!